Silver in the Wood

SILVER
in the
WOOD

EMILY TESH

A TOM DOHERTY ASSOCIATES BOOK

NEW YORK

This is a work of fiction. All of the characters, organizations, and events portrayed in this novella are either products of the author's imagination or are used fictitiously.

SILVER IN THE WOOD

Copyright © 2019 by Emily Tesh

Cover art and design by David Curtis

Edited by Ruoxi Chen

A Tor.com Book
Published by Tom Doherty Associates
175 Fifth Avenue
New York, NY 10010

www.tor.com

Tor® is a registered trademark of
Macmillan Publishing Group, LLC.

ISBN 978-1-250-22978-6 (ebook)
ISBN 978-1-250-22979-3 (trade paperback)

First Edition: June 2019

For Ev
in honour of a conversation we had in your kitchen

I

Emily Tesh

IT WAS THE MIDDLE OF AN AUTUMN DOWNPOUR when Tobias first met Henry Silver. Summer had come and gone, and the wood was quiet. Tobias was snug inside his neat little cottage with Pearl asleep on the hearth, tail twitching occasionally as she dreamed of catching sparrows. He had all his knives laid out in a row on the table and his oilstone to hand. He looked up through the cloudy panes of his one good window and saw the young man in a well-fitted grey coat stumbling along the track with wet leaves blowing into his face and his hat a crumpled ruin in his hands. Then Tobias didn't even really think about it, just stepped outside and hollered for him to come in. The young man looked up with a startled expression. He had a soft boyish face and pale grey eyes, and his mud-coloured hair was plastered to his skin.

"I said come on in, you're getting soaked," called Tobias from his doorway.

The young man stared at him a little longer, and then carefully opened Tobias's garden gate, closed it again behind him, and walked down the path to the cottage. Tobias stood aside to let him in. "Need some help with that coat?" he asked.

"Thank you," said the young man, and once Tobias had taken it off him—it was a damn good coat, even Tobias could tell that, the kind so perfectly tailored it required a servant to pour you into it and peel you out again—he saw that his new guest really was soaked through.

"I'll get you some clothes," he said.

He went into the cottage's one other room and fetched out some of his old things. "I'm Tobias Finch," he said as he came back to the main room. The young man was crouched by the fire. Pearl had opened slitted eyes to consider him, but she was a very unflappable cat, not likely to be startled from her warm spot by a stranger who did not disturb her.

"Silver," said his guest after a moment. "Henry Silver."

"Pleasure's all mine, Mr Silver," said Tobias, and offered him the pile of dry clothes.

Silver got changed and then sat down by the fire again. Pearl graciously crawled into his lap and butted his hand with her head to indicate he might have the honour of petting her. Tobias sat down by the window and returned to sharpening his knives. He let himself glance over once in a while, but Silver didn't seem inclined to chatter and Tobias had never been the talkative type. He often intimidated people, being a big and grim-looking sort of fellow; he'd accepted it years ago and had long since stopped trying to be the kind of man who smiled enough to make up for it. Silver's hair dried into fluffy curls, and although not a particularly small man, he looked like he might disappear inside Tobias's shirt and trousers.

An hour or so went by. Silver stroked the cat, who eventually began to purr. Tobias finished sharpening his knives, put them all away in their proper places, and got out his mending. The rain was still going strong, rattling on the roof and through the trees. An occasional distant boom meant there was thunder in the wind somewhere. "Might go all night," he said at last, owning the truth. "You can have my bed."

"They say a madman lives in Greenhollow Wood," said Silver, looking over at him.

"Who's *they*?" said Tobias.

"The people I spoke to in Hallerton village. They say there's a wild man out here—a priest of the old gods, or a desperate criminal, or just an ordinary lunatic. He eats nothing but meat, raw, and it has made him grow to a giant's stature; or so I was given to understand at the Fox and Feathers. They informed me I would know him by his height and his hair."

"His hair, hmm," said Tobias.

"Waist-length and unwashed," said Silver, looking at Tobias.

"Now that's a slander," said Tobias. "It's not past my elbows, and I wash all over every week."

"I'm glad to hear it, Mr Finch," said Silver.

"The rest's all true," said Tobias.

"Old gods *and* banditry *and* lunacy?"

"And the one where I eat people," said Tobias, unsmiling.

Silver laughed abruptly, a splendid peal of sound. "Maidens, they told me. Yellow-haired for preference."

"Nothing for you to worry about, then," said Tobias. He finished darning his old sock. "I'll make up the bed fresh for you, or as fresh as it'll go."

"You're very kind," said Silver. "You don't even know who I am."

"Figure you must be the new owner up at Greenhallow Hall," said Tobias. "Which makes you my landlord. Not being kind, just buttering you up."

He made up the bed in the other room with the clean set of winter blankets, which he hadn't been planning to get out for another week. The old blankets were stained with moss-green markings. Tobias bundled them up in the corner to wash.

"Are you sure about this?" said Silver when Tobias waved him towards the bed. "Where will you sleep?"

"Floor," said Tobias.

"It doesn't look very comfortable," said Silver. "The

bed's big enough to share, surely." He gave Tobias a smile.

Tobias looked down at him and said, "Really?"

"Well," said Silver, after contemplating the bulk of To-bias for a moment or two, "maybe not."

"I'll be all right. I sleep out by the fire plenty of nights this time of year. Pearl'll keep me company," said Tobias. "Get along to bed with you."

"I'd argue longer but I *am* tired," said Silver. "You must let me make it up to you somehow."

"Cut my rent," said Tobias.

Silver went off to sleep in Tobias's bed in Tobias's shirt, and Pearl treacherously went and joined him, so Tobias sat alone by the fire, not sleeping. As it burned lower and lower, the rain died down to a drizzle, and then it quieted and there was only the gentle drip drip from the leaves of the old oak tree behind the cottage. Tobias took up a newly sharpened knife and trimmed his fingernails. He'd meant to do it earlier, but then Silver had been there. Afterwards he swept up the scattered dry curls of dead leaves and tossed them on the embers.

Sometime after midnight, sitting in the near dark and thinking about nothing very much, Tobias suddenly snorted with laughter. Silver had been *inviting* him, and not just to share a bed that definitely couldn't fit the two of them. How long had it been, if Tobias couldn't even recognise a handsome lad suggesting a bit of mutual entertainment anymore?

A long, long time, that was what. *A long time,* whispered the low rustle of the breeze in the leaves outside. *A long time,* sang the drip-drip-drip of rainwater, softly, while Tobias sat clear-eyed and sleepless in the dark, listening to the wood.

~

In the morning, Silver thanked him and bade him farewell cheerfully enough. Tobias pointed out the road to the Hall and handed him his clothes, dry and not too weather-stained, to change back into. "Heaven knows what the housekeeper will think," said Silver, "when I tell her I spent the night with the wild man in the woods."

"She'll have the reverend come and visit to check you over for black magic, most likely," said Tobias.

Silver laughed as if he'd been joking. "Thank you again for your hospitality," he said. Then he was striding off into the woodland. Tobias watched him go, trim in his good coat, hatless and light-footed among the leaves. A nice young fellow, certainly.

He finished his mending that morning, and rehung the cottage door that had swollen in the rain, and went looking for mistletoe. The old oak obliged him as usual, but more never hurt, and Tobias had learned over the years it was worth his time to walk the woods after a rainstorm. He went down to the gully where the stream ran quick, up to the edge of the hills, skirted round the village, and checked the old shrine. It was looking pretty ragged since they'd built the village church, but someone had left a handful of blackberries. Tobias ate them one by one as he went to take a look at the woodsmen's copse. The chief there knew his work, so there were no problems. They'd set up a crossed circle of white stones facing east, casual-looking enough to fool a priest, but there wasn't much power in it. More of a habit than a protection, these days. Still, Tobias appreciated the gesture. It made his work easier.

The woods had been cut back around the Hall back in the year ten, and Tobias couldn't get close, but he stood at the edge of the pretty garden they'd laid out and eyed the old building with its dark windows. Silver was a nice fellow. Tobias didn't regret inviting him in out of the rain.

He didn't find any more mistletoe in the end, but really the oak's offering was enough. He went back to his cottage, fixed himself some dinner, strapped on his knives, and oiled his crossbow. A sprig of mistletoe in his belt, clean socks with darned heels, good boots, and he was ready.

He'd found the trail a few days ago up on the hills, among the twisted gorse. It was a sad thing when a dryad went sour. They were sweet ladies for the most part, and Tobias liked them. He had four or five in his wood, not counting the old oak, who was his own manner of thing. This one wasn't a local; she smelled rootless and angry. Lost her tree, most likely, and no one had asked her mercy or planted her a sapling. She'd go for the woodsmen, who slept in a long cabin just outside the village. Damn thing was wooden, which wouldn't make Tobias's task any easier.

He took up a station on the edge of the copse just before moonrise and waited.

It took her a long time to get there. More than half the night was through by the time she arrived, and she'd missed the midnight hour, when she would have been strongest. "How now," Tobias murmured when he saw her swell into being on the edge of the clearing. She was twisted and reddish, and her eyes lacked the sunlight-in-the-canopy gleam of a healthy dryad. "Now then, miss," Tobias said. "There's no call for this."

She hissed at him.

"Why don't you come along with me," said Tobias, "and we'll plant you a sweet willow, down by the river, with water to sing to you and sun on your leaves?"

The dryad swayed and muttered. Tobias didn't have much hope for her. There was a dry rotted scent rolling off her; she was in no mood to put down roots. Her dim eyes were fixed on the cabin full of sleeping men. "Now, miss," said Tobias gently all the same. "No need for anyone to get hurt."

"*Them,*" hissed the dryad.

"They're good woodsmen, miss. I watch 'em myself. They cut clean and plant after. No shame in being builders, miss, and it's a nice little copse. What do you say to that willow, now?"

"They killed me," moaned the dryad, swaying on the spot. There was a deep rumbling sound under her words. Tobias stopped hoping. She was older and madder than he'd thought. "They killed me, and I—"

She screamed. The timbers of the cabin all shook with the sound.

Tobias quickly raised his crossbow. The bolt made a solid *thunk* as it lodged in her dim eye. She howled again, and the undergrowth shifted and sprouted pale vines that snatched for Tobias's legs. She'd forget her victims till she was done with him.

Most of the grasping vines changed their mind about Tobias when they touched his boots. This was his wood, and one uprooted dryad—even a strong old one—couldn't turn it against him all at once. He drew one of his knives, plain steel with a good edge, to hack apart the few that kept coming. The dryad screamed and screamed the whole time. She was putting herself into the vines to make them attack him, spending the last of her ancient strength to do it. Tobias advanced on her slowly and steadily, reaching for the mistletoe sprig in his belt as he came. She stumbled back before him and stepped straight into the crossed circle of white stones the woodsmen had set up. They blazed with pale light, and in that gleam Tobias finally got a good look at her. She was ruddy-skinned for autumn and there were still some withered flowers in her dried-out papery hair. The stone circle had her trapped now. Poor creature, Tobias thought.

He put another crossbow bolt in her. The force of it snapped something inside her; she shuddered and fell, straight and heavy in the way of her kind, with a creaking noise. "Rest well," Tobias said, standing over her. He laid the mistletoe sprig over her heart and brought his old flint blade down through it.

She wailed one last time, a winter-wind shriek of rattling boughs, and died. Tobias sighed. He turned around to check on the cabin.

The door was open, and half a dozen men were crowding out of it staring at him. Before Tobias had time to say anything, one of them lifted a pistol and fired it.

His hands were shaking, which surely saved Tobias's life, that and the dark of the night. Tobias clenched his teeth around a yell when the bullet went into his thigh.

Time went slow around him, heavy and green after the way of the trees, and he saw the trembling man with the pistol try to aim again. Probably never killed anyone in his life, Tobias thought. Probably thinks he's being a hero. What could the woodsmen see, after all, but the wild man coming for them, and the hideous tangle of the dryad's death throes?

The slow green time carried on pooling around Tobias's feet, and the pain of the wound felt distant through it. Tobias lurched away into the trees and limped as fast as he could go towards his cottage. Bracken brushed itself out of his way and low branches moved aside. He caught sight of a slim figure in the trees off to his left; golden-eyed like all her kind, but moving swift, so she was Bramble, the youngest of Tobias's dryads and the one with the nastiest temper. "Leave 'em be, miss," he said to her.

"You're hurt!" she cried.

"They'll hack you back to a stump if you're foolish," Tobias said. He was stumbling now, but his cottage and the old oak were looming ahead, both much closer to the woodland's edge than they usually were. "I've had worse. Leave people things to people, dear heart."

She cried out in protest, but she didn't go off to chase down the silly youth with the pistol, so that was something. Tobias lurched into his cottage and time abruptly poured itself back into its proper shape. He saw the shadows settle over the floor as Bramble took up a guard all around the place, calling up blackthorn and dark holly on every side, planting herself by the door in a menacing tangle. Well, there went Tobias's vegetable garden.

The hole in his leg was bleeding sluggishly. Tobias washed it out with yarrow, wincing at the sting. Then he bound it up in clean bandages and went and lay down on the bed without getting any more undressed than that. Pearl came and sat by him, lashing her tail silently. Tobias closed his eyes. Time went slow and green around him again, and the pain fell back a little.

Bullet lodged in his thigh, and he was no doctor; nor was anything that lived in his wood. Well, there it was. He'd live or not. If he lived, he'd manage, and if he died, he'd die in the shadow of the old oak. Maybe it was time. He'd seen nearly four hundred summers come and go by now.

He kept his eyes closed and tried to go to sleep.

~

"Finch! Finch! Where are you? Finch!"

The cry was coming from somewhere outside. Tobias groaned softly as time sped up again to let him hear it. The wound in his thigh was aching, and not with the dull throb of healing pain. Who was disturbing him now? Hell, who was there left who even knew his name?

One person: and summer had already been and gone. Tobias closed his eyes.

"Mr Finch!" came the cry again, and the swearing of someone who'd got his coat caught on a thorn bush. "How on earth—"

Bramble's sunlit eyes peered in at Tobias's wavering window, a dull cat gleam through the thick glass. Past holly and blackthorn Tobias caught a glimpse of mud-coloured curls and a grey coat. It was Silver, of course. Of course Silver knew his name.

"Hullo?" called Silver. "Hullo?"

He wouldn't find the cottage unless the wood let him, not if he searched for a hundred years: he could stand right outside the door yelling and not see it. Bramble's slow blink at Tobias through the glass said: *Shall I throw him in a ditch?*

"No," muttered Tobias, and winced when the effort made his leg scream at him again. "No, let him in."

"Wh—oh!" he heard a moment later, and then Silver was knocking on his door. He didn't wait for Tobias to invite him inside this time, which was just as well. Tobias didn't think he had the strength to make the words. "I must have walked right past the place," Tobias heard him say as he came into the main room, and then he was standing over the bed somehow. He moved fast, Silver, or else Tobias was worse off than he thought. "I heard a story in Hallerton about how they'd chased off the wild man with a pistol," Silver said, staring down at him. "I came to see if— My God."

He'd seen the bloodstain under Tobias's thigh.

"My God," whispered Silver again, and he stared down at Tobias, and put out a hand as if he meant to touch him. It hovered over the wounded leg, then over Tobias's shoulder, then near his forehead, but never reached all the way. "Have you been lying here three days? What if you'd— Heaven help us, did you mean to bleed out alone in the woods? Do you hate the company of your fellows that much?"

Tobias said nothing, because speaking seemed very difficult. Time would not slow with another person here. The wood could not take him out of this moment. Bramble was still glaring in through the window, watchful. Tobias knew she would have come inside to crowd threateningly up against Silver's shoulder and put more tears in his coat if she could.

"I'm not having it," Silver said. "You're my tenant. I'll pay for the doctor. You must have a doctor. And be moved; this place isn't fit for a wounded man. My God! What were those trigger-happy fools in the coppice doing? Did they take you for a thief?"

He did not seem to expect an answer, which was just as well.

"We'll have you safe at Greenhollow Hall in no time," he said, and this time his hand did reach Tobias's shoulder, and held it firmly for a moment. "Within the hour, if I can manage it."

~

When Tobias next woke, he was lying on a bed as soft as moss and as cool as fresh water, and the throb in his leg was a steady healing pounding, not the slow burn of infection and death. He knew at once that he would be well again.

There was a breeze from an open window, blowing the smell of freshly cut grass into the little room, and Pearl was lying on the end of his bed with her paws stretched out, totally at her ease. Tobias tried to sit up and failed. When he turned his head, he was aware of an odd heaviness which confused him until he realised: they'd washed his hair and plaited it. No doubt someone had found him offensively untidy until then. The heart of Tobias's untidiness wouldn't be fixed by any washing. Already there were brackish stains on the bed linen.

He did not recognise the room he was lying in, but then there was no reason he should; the Hall had been through a score of owners and at least two fires since Tobias had last set foot inside it. It was a plain room, but the kind of plain that had strength behind it: brick and plaster, high ceilings, heavy furniture. There was an ewer on a small table by the bed. Tobias was thirsty, but if he tried to reach for it now he'd just knock it down. Someone would come in by and by. No one got put in a bed like this in a room like this and then just left there.

"Ah, Mr Finch," said Silver when he came in, and he smiled. "I'm glad to see you looking well."

Tobias just looked at him.

"Water?" said Silver. When Tobias nodded, Silver came and sat on the edge of the bed to pour him some and hold the cup for him while he drank. Tobias felt weak as a child. Some of that was his injury; the rest lay in how far he'd come from the wood. He could only feel a trace of it, out at the edges of the Hall's gardens.

"I'm afraid I've had to break our bargain," Silver said.

"What?"

"To cut your rent," said Silver. "I would have done it, very gladly, but I had a look through the Hall's records and it's a funny thing. You don't seem to pay any."

Tobias said nothing.

"The last mention of the woodland cottage is some four hundred years ago, in fact," said Silver. "Can you believe that? It seems the Rafelas just forgot about the place. So I'm terribly sorry, but in order to explain your presence here to the doctor I'm afraid I've had to *raise* your rent. You pay it in service now."

Tobias still kept silent.

"I don't want you to think that I'm—that is, I'm not going to ask you any questions," said Silver, "along the lines of *what are you doing in my wood* and so on."

Tobias snorted at that.

"What? Oh, my wood. Yes, I know," said Silver, "I've only been here a few months."

"It's yours in the law all the same," Tobias said.

"And no doubt you know every nook of it and think the law can go hang itself," Silver said. "Which is just as well, because, you see, if anyone asks, you're my game-keeper. I had to explain you somehow. 'Wild man' just wasn't going to satisfy my mother."

"Your mother?"

"She somehow knows everything," said Silver, "and she writes the most horrible letters. I couldn't risk her coming down in person. She'd tell me I had to make my employees cut their hair."

"Well," said Tobias, "we wouldn't want that."

"No indeed," said Silver. He ducked his head and gave Tobias a small smile. "I don't believe I could make you do it in any case. You are quite a lot bigger than I am."

"I'm a wounded man," said Tobias.

"You insult me. I wouldn't bring scissors to bear on an invalid."

"Only way you'd have a chance," said Tobias. He pictured it, Silver taking scissors to Tobias's shaggy head. He'd have a hard time of it. Be better off with garden shears.

Silver covered his face with his hands. "I know!" Then he peered between his fingers at Tobias. "Forgive me, I am a poor comforter for invalids. I should say: how are you feeling?"

Tobias thought about it. He could not say to Silver: *like a thing uprooted*, though he was. It was sure that without Silver and his gamekeeper story and the doctor he'd plainly paid for, Tobias would be dead. "Better," he said in the end. "Could do with some more sleep."

Silver stood at once. "I won't prevent it," he said. "There's a bell on the table. Ring it if you need anything, anything at all. I am eccentric, and all the servants have grown resigned to it. I may indulge my gamekeeper if I wish."

"Do you hunt?" said Tobias abruptly.

Silver made a face. "Never. I haven't the stomach for it. Don't worry, I shan't expect any actual gamekeeping from you."

Tobias nodded.

"Sleep, sleep!" said Silver. "Sleep well. Don't worry. I've managed everything."

Tobias slept. He only woke up a handful of times in the next week, usually when Silver came in to give him some water. Once Silver tried to give him laudanum. Tobias could smell the poppy. He roused enough to spit it out. "I didn't want you to be in pain," said Silver, confused and put out. "The doctor said . . ."

"Hang the doctor," growled Tobias.

He was ashamed after for losing his temper. He always tried not to: it seemed to him that being a big fellow meant you had to keep a rein on yourself. But he was beginning to get restless, lying in a bed all day with nothing to do except wait for Silver to come in and take a look at him.

"Sorry," he said, next time Silver came to see him, the following morning.

"What? Oh, the laudanum! No, no, I'm the one who should be sorry," Silver said. "I should have asked you if you wanted it first. I hope there's not some history, or . . ."

The inquiry hung there. Tobias had known Silver was curious, had seen him bite his tongue on it half a dozen times. This was the first time the curiosity had made it to the surface. Tobias wasn't going to encourage it. "None," he said. "Just don't like the stuff." It was even true. "Shouldn't have lost my temper. Fidgety, is all."

"Of course, of course, you're bored," said Silver. "That's good news! It must mean you're healing. Perhaps a book?"

Tobias snorted.

Silver looked embarrassed. "Oh, I thought—there's a school in Hallerton, and these days—not that there's anything wrong with—" He caught his breath. "If you have never had the opportunity to learn to read, Mr Finch," he said, "I should be delighted to teach you."

"Had the opportunity," said Tobias. "Just not the knack. Never got any good at it." He took pity on Silver's embarrassment. "Wouldn't mind hearing some tales, though. You could read to me."

Silver went a little pink. "I'd be delighted," he said.

After that he turned up at Tobias's sickbed every evening with a little leather-bound volume. He had a pleasant voice for listening to, one that went up and down soothingly. Tobias didn't always pay attention to the words. It was nice to hear a human voice speaking, the rises and falls of it.

~

A week or so of that went by, and Tobias felt well enough to rise out of bed and stomp around, stare out the window towards the dark shades of the wood on the edge of the park. He couldn't stay here much longer.

"So what're you doing at the Hall?" he asked Silver that night, interrupting the sweet up-and-down of his voice as he read through a book of folklore. It was all old village tales, country stories written down in stern professorial language, strange stuff. Silver jerked when Tobias interrupted. Come to think of it, Tobias hadn't been doing much talking, these nights. Just listening, to the hills and valleys of Silver's voice. Watching the candlelight on his curls. Wasn't a surprise that Tobias had forgotten how to make conversation, but Silver must have been out of the habit of expecting it from him.

"Well," Silver said after he was done looking startled, and he laid the book down open on his lap. "This, if I'm honest. Though you mustn't tell my mother." The way Silver talked, his mother was little short of an ogress.

"This?"

"Folklore," said Silver. "Studying—investigating. Of course I'm not a *real* scholar." He said this as if Tobias might have challenged him on it. "But so much of our heritage is disappearing in this day and age. The costs of progress. I'm interested in preserving what I can."

"Get boys and girls from the village in the woods sometimes," said Tobias. "Running about with nets. Catching butterflies."

"That's exactly it," said Silver, breaking out in a big

grin. "I'm catching butterflies. In any case, Greenhollow Wood has a fascinating set of local legends swirling around it. The Wild Man story is a case in point. I spoke to your attacker, by the way. Charlie Bondee, woodsman. He feels quite the fool and is desperate to apologise. When he saw you there in the night, he really did believe the spirit of the wood had come to assault the village."

"Did he now," said Tobias, smiling. The smile was as much for Silver's butterfly-catching grin as it was for the woodsman with the pistol. Poor Charlie Bondee.

"You must admit, Mr Finch," said Silver, "you are an alarming-looking fellow."

The way he said it, and the look he gave Tobias with it, was flirting. Flirting! At least Tobias recognised it this time. Funny thing, to be flirted with by a pretty young fellow who wore expensive coats. Made Tobias feel young again, and at the same time very, very old.

He didn't answer because he had no answer for it. Instead he smiled, and shook his head, and Silver took it as gracefully as if he had never been looking at Tobias's hair and hands and shoulders in the first place. "Perhaps you'd like to know more about the Wild Man of Greenhollow Wood?" he said. "You never know; you might meet him someday. You are living in his domain, after all."

"Go on, then," said Tobias, and Silver leaned forward in his chair as he began to tell the local stories he'd been researching. He had a funny way of talking when he hadn't the book to keep him on track: he kept cutting himself off to explain things, theorise, and remark about similar stories he'd heard elsewhere. "The Wild or Green Man figure comes up over and over in this part of the country," he said at one point, "and is obviously the modern interpretation of one of the so-called 'old gods,' a tutelary spirit or woodland demigod. I think the myth is separate from—although similar to—to the myths of the Fairy King, because regardless of the Wild Man's particular interpretation—whether aggressive or generous, a savage enemy of civilisation or its protector—he never has a *court* and is always fundamentally *alone*: a primitive figure, not from a different civilisation but from before civilisation existed at all. Whereas the Fairy King—"

It was a lot of nonsense. No such thing as a fairy king, so far as Tobias knew, and by now he'd probably have come across one if there was one to find. Fairies he had met, and chased off usually; even more than dryads, they were better off far away from humans, and humans far from them. But the nonsense made it easier for Tobias to be amused by the whole thing: lying in a soft white bed, with his wood too far away, listening to old wives' tales of himself.

∼

Before long the boredom of the white room and the soft bed was more than Tobias could bear. He didn't like the feeling of being trapped. In his wood, he could step out of the cottage any time of the day or night and tramp away under the trees, down as far as the boundary stones of Hallerton or all the way out east to the boggy wetland there.

One morning he got himself up and went out into the house.

At first he limped along lost, turning corners and trying shiny brass doorknobs without any idea what was behind them. He leaned on the walls when he had to give his bad leg a rest. They were high and strong and brick-and-mortar, more human than Tobias was used to. But he came through a double set of doors and out into a big room with a stone fireplace, and then he knew the place, of course. This was the heart of the Hall.

They'd put a new roof on it. Tobias tipped his head back to look at it. He'd used to knock his head on the doorframes, walking this way. Hadn't happened once this morning.

A young woman at work on the flagstones with a scrubbing brush and a bucket of soapy water gave him a nervous look. Tobias nodded gravely at her and stomped carefully away through the doors on the far side of the room.

It was still the library. It looked a little different. Dark polished shelves shone in the light from the big glass windows. There were scores, no, hundreds of books arrayed along them. In the middle of the room was a table, the same dark-shining fine-grained timber that Tobias didn't recognise—so nothing that had ever grown in *his* wood—with maps and journals and a dozen heavy tomes spread on it.

Silver was up a ladder. "Mr Finch!" he cried from overhead. He scrambled down and jumped the last few rungs. No coat on him this morning, and pale eyes full of light when he smiled. "I'm so glad to see you up and about," he said. "What can I do for you?" He frowned. "Sit, sit down. I'm sure you shouldn't walk too far on that leg just yet."

He ushered Tobias into a high-backed chair before Tobias could object. It was big enough to take all Tobias's bulk without a creak. Silver smiled at him and said, "I take it the fidgets were too much for you?"

"You're working," said Tobias.

"I'm always happy to have company. Especially if it's a captive audience," Silver said.

He meant it, too. Tobias leaned back in the chair, which was near as comfortable as the soft bed, and watched him dart around his polished bookshelves, pulling down this book and that one. He talked to Tobias the whole time, explaining what he was doing though Tobias barely recognised the things he knew, the dryads and nightwalkers and places of power, in Silver's cheery brookwater babble. He only spoke once, to ask about the timber.

"Oh—mahogany—I think?" said Silver. "It's the done thing." He looked around as if he was only just seeing it. "It is rather lovely, I suppose."

"Aye," said Tobias.

Silver went back to his flicking through books and chattering. Seemed a funny sort of way to do work to Tobias, but Silver looked pleased with himself. "Green-hollow was an important site," he said, "there's no doubt about that in my mind at all. The old gods *mattered* here. Now tracing the exact preoccupations of a preliterate society is tricky, of course, but the landscape itself bears witness, so if you look at the maps—"

He had four or five spread across the table. Tobias levered himself to his feet and let Silver take his arm to point at them. It took him a moment to make sense of them, but once he saw the picture he didn't need Silver to say "—and this is eighteenth-century, and this is sixteenth, and this is a reconstruction based on what records we have from the twelfth—"

Tobias nodded. He knew the shape of his own wood.

"You can see the typical disregard for spelling conventions, of course," Silver said. "Cartographers have settled on *Greenhollow* in the present day, but it's just as often spelled *hallow* right up to the turn of the century, sometimes one word and sometimes two. One assumes the pronunciation changed over time."

"I can see that, can I?" Tobias said.

Silver blushed, but then he glanced up at Tobias with a little grin. Liked his work, this one. "Well," he said, "you'll have to take my word for it."

Tobias said nothing, just raised his brows.

"Now *this*," Silver said, unrolling another paper, "is my own work."

Tobias frowned down at it. "That the wood?" he said.

It was. It was absolutely the wood. The shape of it fit cleanly into Tobias's mind. But there was no sign of the village, only a mark of a crossed circle where the shrine ought to be. The Hall was missing as well, the green mass of the wood spreading freely over the land where it would be and off towards the edge of the map. It rolled away in every direction, even up over the hills and angling fingers out into the wetland. "When's that, then?" he said.

"At least three thousand years ago," said Silver. "Maybe more. There are known barrows here and here"—pointing to neat crosses drawn amongst the hills—"and more in this direction, if you see. The course of Haller Brook has changed substantially, of course, so some of this is really a guess. But this is the primaeval forest. The modern Greenhollow is only a remnant of a sacred space that was much, much greater. I call it the Hallow Wood."

Tobias nodded slowly as he looked down at it. "Suppose that makes sense," he said. He nearly reached out to touch, but Silver's map was fine work on fine paper, and he didn't trust his own rough hands.

Silver looked up from the map to Tobias's face and smiled at whatever he saw. "Do you think so?" he said, all warm pleasure. "I'm glad."

~

Tobias went back to his cottage a few days later. Silver wrung his hands about it, but now Tobias could walk, he couldn't linger. He needed to be back under the old oak, and Bramble would be worrying.

"I will be visiting," said Silver. "The doctor said you had to rest, Mr Finch, and I mean to see that his orders are followed."

"Don't plan to go out adventuring," said Tobias, honestly. The wood could take care of itself a little while. "Just want to be in my own bed."

Silver gave him a walking stick, and Tobias set off in the morning and walked across the Hall's pretty gardens towards the dark blot of the trees. Every step he took closer to the forest made him feel stronger: by the time he could make out the blackberry tangles at the wood's edge, he barely needed the walking stick at all. Bramble was waiting for him, sunlit eyes unblinking as she curled among her thorns. "I'm here, my dear," said Tobias, and crossed into the shadow of the trees.

At once slow deep green rolled over him. He took a breath, and another, smelling old rotting leaves and healthy growth and autumn light. He felt almost as though he could have planted his feet and become a tree himself, a strong oak reaching up to the sky, brother of the old oak who ruled the wood. Ah, he thought, and nothing else. Silver and his mud-coloured curls and silly stories seemed a dim faraway thing. Ah, the wood.

Whatever else happened, no matter how many summers he endured, Tobias had this.

He took up the walking stick he was still holding, and looked at it a moment, and then planted it firmly in the good soil under his feet. He felt it take root, that old dead wood, and the carvings undid themselves as it sprouted every way. Bramble came and stood by him and blinked at it, and then she put her hands out and put some of her own strength into it, real dryad's strength, and ten minutes later there was a sapling standing there.

"Thanks," said Tobias.

Bramble kissed his cheek, leaving a red scratch behind.

Tobias went home to his cottage.

It was good to be home, and quiet, with the trees all about him. It was the wrong time of year for Tobias to re-plant the vegetable garden Bramble had ruined in her fit of protectiveness, but he had plenty to get him through the winter. Pearl dozed on his bed all day and hunted by night. Tobias stayed in, letting his leg heal and listening to the wood. All was calm. No more stray dryads. Every-thing gone still and chill, waiting, all winter long. The wood knew as well as Tobias did what would come back with the sun.

He let Silver come to see him a time or two, took care to have his cottage in the same place every time. Braided his hair when he felt Silver's tread snapping careless twigs on the forest's edge. No reason to do that, but he'd got in the habit of having it out of his face, maybe, those weeks in that soft bed up at the Hall. Silver carried on chasing his butterflies. One day he took Tobias to see the old shrine and pointed out the evidence that despite all modern developments some people were still leaving of-ferings. "You can clearly see the stains," he said with sat-isfaction. "Some sort of blood sacrifice—"

"Or blackberry juice," said Tobias, hiding a smile. "Stains everything, that does."

Silver subsided. Nothing very exciting about blackber-ries, Tobias supposed. Hadn't been any new offerings since autumn anyway. Couple of times a year was the best Tobias hoped for, really. Occasionally something on a solstice.

Another time Silver brought the woodsman Charlie Bondee to see him. Poor lad was dying of embarrassment and couldn't apologise enough for his quick shot. "It was only," he said, "when I saw ye, Master Finch—"

"Did me no harm in the end, and all's well, as they say," said Tobias firmly.

"If you'd grown up round here, you'd know," said Charlie, "and I know well enough it's only an old story, but when you loomed up out of the dark, as it were, with all your hair and all—"

"Never mind! Never mind!" Tobias said.

"I hope you see, Mr Bondee," said Silver sternly, "the dangers of superstition." He sounded like a schoolmaster. Couldn't have been more than a year older than Charlie.

"Oh yes! Yes!" said Charlie.

"There's a lot of interesting stories about Greenhollow Wood, I know," said Silver. "But that's all they are—folktales. There are no dryads, no wild men, no fairy kings, and no monsters. Isn't that right, Mr Finch?"

"Certainly haven't seen a fairy king yet," said Tobias.

Charlie went away still embarrassed. Tobias gave Silver a steady look. "There was no call for that, now," he said. "Poor lad meant no harm."

"A young man who means no harm should not be

firing pistols," said Silver.

Tobias shrugged. "I still say all's well that ends well."

Silver laughed suddenly. "Of course you do. You must be the most forgiving man alive."

~

It was getting close to midwinter. Silver disappeared for a while, gone to stay with his ogress mother. Tobias, finally healed up as well as he was going to be, took a mistletoe sprig and his flint knife and laid a ghoul to rest up among the barrows on the hills the night before the new year. Bramble accompanied him. She didn't let him go out alone any longer, and followed him through the woods, sprouting curtains of thorns wherever she went. "It was only once, my darling," Tobias said, exasperated.

Bramble smiled, showing her sharp brown teeth. "Miss," she said. "Not miss?"

"You can't call a lass miss when she trails you everywhere," Tobias said. "This isn't proper dryad doings, my dear. You should go plant yourself. Grow big and tall like your sisters."

"Is that what you did?" said Bramble. "You are much bigger than any other human. Did you plant yourself?"

Tobias caught his breath on a painful laugh. "Not exactly," he said. "But maybe that's close enough."

~

Wildflowers began to spring up in the woods around the same time Silver came back. Tobias let Bramble tuck some into his hair one morning, and then forgot they were there until after Silver had already visited him and gone again. He hadn't said a word.

Tobias tried to enjoy spring the way the dryad did. Hard to stick to it. The equinox was coming: still a few months away, but Tobias woke every day with the sunrise, aware of what was coming as it came year on year.

And then Silver heard the story.

"The bandits of Greenhollow Wood," he said with satisfaction, sitting before the fire one evening. "I doubt you know this one. It's apparently very seldom told. But it's a fascinating little mix of myth, legend, and local history. You know the Hall?" He did not wait for an answer. "I purchased it from an agent for the family that used to own it, and he never mentioned the story—which is unusual, these people normally try to throw in a little local colour—but then I wrote to Lady Rafela, and her reply reached me last week. She'd never heard it before either, but she went to the family records and apparently that branch of cousins was mentioned several times in connection with some *great shame*. It all fits! Heavens, I'm sorry, I've started in the wrong place. I must sound like a perfect loon."

"Take a deep breath," Tobias advised. He tried to think about Silver's bright enthusiasm, his pale eyes sparkling under the fall of his brown curls, rather than about the story. He knew the story. Of course he did.

"Fabian Rafela," Silver said, giving the name a proper sonorous spin that Tobias hadn't heard for centuries. "Or *Red Fay,* as he was known. The connection to the local fairy legends is obvious, and no doubt he found it convenient. As far as I can tell, the actual facts of the matter are that he was a local baron who gathered himself a little band of thugs during a lean winter and took to raiding to supplement his income. A nasty piece of work and nothing more. But the *stories,* Mr Finch!"

Yes, thought Tobias. The stories.

The way Silver told it wasn't quite right. It had been four hundred years, and people had been adding things to it. Red Fay went into the woods one day and met a fairy prince—well, that wasn't altogether true, but close enough, Tobias guessed. He was offered three wishes in return for his soul. (*A very traditional motif,* Silver said, excited.) He wished for riches, and beauty, and immortality. Thereafter he terrorised all the people around and about with his robber band for many a year, stealing whatever pleased him, never losing a fight. At last the day came when the fairy prince came back for his soul, and then Red Fay met his comeuppance.

Ah, Fabian, with his long copper braid, his sweet smile, his brilliant eyes! No need to wish for beauty, that one; and riches he'd preferred to win for himself.

Immortality, though. The wood could give you that, after a manner of speaking. And it had, after all, been Fabian Rafela's wood.

~

Silver grew obsessed with the bandit story. He kept coming back to Tobias with more details, more things he'd read up or heard about. He must have interviewed every grandmother for ten miles around the wood. Tobias listened quietly to his burbling. When it got to be too much, he tried to stop hearing the words and hear only the rolling landscape of Silver's voice. "You ever sing?" he said abruptly the day Silver came to him fresh from a visit to the magistrate's office in High Lockham and the list of names in the record book. *Thomas de Carre, Simon Simms, John Hunter, John Cooper, Nathan leClerc,* hanged all in a row four hundred years ago.

"What?" said Silver, thrown off his grisly recitation. "That was the whole gang, apparently, apart from Rafela himself and his lieutenant, who fled into the woods to escape the soldiers—I'm sorry, what did you say?"

"Never mind," said Tobias.

But Silver had gone pink. His curls were getting longer and starting to hang in ringlets round his soft face. He was a good-looking fellow. Not beautiful like Fabian, but who was? "I, er," he said, "well, I *can* sing. Did you want . . ."

Tobias shrugged. "Not a lot of music in the wood," he said.

He'd only meant it to throw Silver off his storytelling, and it succeeded in that, so he was taken aback when Silver came to see him next time carrying a—hell, Tobias didn't even know the name. Some kind of stringed instrument. "I thought you might like to hear some folk songs," Silver said, blushing a sweet rose colour.

"Hm," said Tobias, trying not to laugh. "Suppose I would."

Turned out Silver *could* sing. He had a fine, clear voice, a steady voice that made Tobias think of good strong wood grown straight and tall under the sun. In the corner of his eye he could see Bramble pressing up against the shutters as she listened. Silver looked down at his fingers as he plucked the strings, and the rose-pink colour never left his face while he sang. The songs were old ones. Tobias knew most of the tunes, though not all the words. He was enjoying it, truly enjoying it and not thinking of anything else, feeling like a man and not something from under the old oak, when Silver said, "And this one's from the village," and launched into Bloody-Handed Toby.

It was a punch in the gut. The tune was the same Nathan had used to whistle, and the words were mostly the ones the Jacks had come up with, less a couple of the dirtier verses. Silver's voice was wrong for it, but Tobias could barely hear him anymore. He stared into the fire, watching the jumping flames, and heard Fabian again: Fabian's high warbling tenor, cracking and off-key, and his sweet smile and his eyes full of friendly mockery.

The spring equinox was three days off. They would be hanging up bunting and practising the children's parade in the village by now. It happened every year, and had for four hundred years, and for the first time in all those years Tobias had let himself forget about it.

He managed to compliment Silver's singing when it was over. Silver eyed him curiously. Clever fellow, Tobias thought with a sudden bitter fondness. Clever, generous, good-looking fellow, who kept coming back to show Tobias the stories he'd found like a child with a butterfly trapped in a jar.

"Happens I know a story about the wood myself," he said.

Silver sat up a little straighter. "You do?"

"You talked to people down in Hallerton about the festival?"

"The Spring Fair," said Silver at once. "Common all

over the country—a remnant of an older celebration, obviously, presumably in honour of fertility and the sowing season, with the associated old god—goddess, I suppose."

Tobias smiled despite himself. Trust Silver. "Goddess, as a rule, used to be. But round here," he said, "they do it for the Lord of Summer."

Silver blinked at him. "I haven't heard that name. Is he a lesser deity—or perhaps a fairy lord?"

Tobias shrugged. "He's a prince of the season," he said. "Dangerous. Turns up in spring, roams all summer. He needs to be put off; that's what the festival's for."

"Put off?" said Silver. "So this, er, lord of summer, objects to celebrations?"

"No, no, he loves them," said Tobias. "They distract him, you see. Keep him amused with drink and song and games, and he won't be any trouble. It's when he gets bored that the trouble starts."

For Silver's curious look he outlined some of what was meant by *trouble*: the cruel tricks, the unlucky accidents, the stolen treasures. Silver had his eyebrows raised. When Tobias reached the missing lads and lasses he leaned forward in his seat. "Are you *sure* he's not a fairy lord?" he said. "This sounds very much like the fairy myths I've read about elsewhere."

"Not children," explained Tobias. Fairies took children, sometimes, and then didn't know what to do with them; he'd recovered a few in his time, starving and mud-stained, from their baffled and angry kidnappers. "Youths, young folk—unmarried and handsome. He takes them off into the woods and they're never seen again."

"I noticed preparations for a number of weddings in the village," said Silver.

Tobias nodded. "Get 'em married before Summer shows up, and he's no danger to them," he said. "They'll all clasp hands over the fire at the Fair. Lucky time of year to be wed in any case."

Silver smiled. "Perhaps you and I should have found ourselves brides by now, for safety's sake."

"I'm too old," said Tobias.

"You're not as old as all that, Mr Finch."

Tobias shook his head. "But you're his sort of meat, sure enough," he said. "Better to stay away while Summer's abroad. Keep out of the wood and out of his sight."

Silver's eyebrows went up again. "Mr Finch," he said, "I know you are very familiar with these woods. Do you believe there's something to this tale?"

Tobias said nothing.

"I know that the supernatural is considered out of date," said Silver, "and much of what I study is pure superstition and rank nonsense; but I am an open-minded sort of man, you know, and I am always eager to learn. Have you perhaps seen something in Greenhollow to cause you this much concern?"

He was leaning forward; there was a sparkle in his eye despite the seriousness of his tone. Tobias had no doubt that whatever he said next was getting written down in that little notebook, pinned on the page like a winged thing dying. His own cowardice jumped up and choked him. "Not at all," he said, when he should have told the truth. "Only stories. But do a foolish old fellow a favour and stay away for a week or two."

Silver laughed. "If I didn't know better," he said, "I'd think you were trying to get rid of me."

Tobias walked him to the woodland's border on the edge of the Hall's gardens that night, which he never did as a rule. "Good night, Mr Finch," said Silver, looking up at him through his long lashes.

Tobias nodded. He didn't reply. He stood silent in the shade of a tall elm tree with one hand gripping tight around the other behind his back as he watched Silver walk across the lawn. When his little shadowy figure was swallowed up in the great shadow of the house Tobias turned to Bramble. "Don't let him back in," he said. "Tell your sisters. That one's not to walk the woods till the moon comes round again."

Bramble let out a low susurrus of distress. She was

strong, but it was tree-strength, patience and slow growth, and the thing that was waking in Greenhallow by the week's end was beyond her power to restrain for the same reason it was beyond Tobias's.

"Aye, lass," said Tobias. "I know. Just don't let Silver near, and I'll deal with Fabian."

"You never have," said Bramble. "You never could."

"Don't worry, my darling," Tobias said, "Don't worry about me."

He went back to his cottage and sat down with his back against the old oak. Sometimes he wondered if the tree felt sorry for him. A kind of nonsense. The tree was a tree; he felt tree-things, sunlight and earth and so on, and Tobias was only another kind of thing that dwelt upon him, no different if you thought about it from the squirrel's nest in the nook of the trunk. Dryads might feel—no doubt Bramble was fond of Tobias—oh, all sorts of old things from the wood might feel, but it seemed to him they felt differently to mortals. Bramble could be fond, could be angry; fairies managed envy and pride easily enough; old rotting hunger-things that came out of the bogs and crept in among the willow-groves to the east felt a terrible desire, but to feel as mortals felt—to laugh as mortals laughed, and look up under the eyelashes, and sing old songs to the plucked strings of a whatever-it-was—

Tobias was a fool and always had been.

He groaned and stood up. When he looked up he found it was pitchy dark. Time had softened around him the way it so often did. Maybe that was the wood's version of pity.

~

Tobias sharpened all his knives, and darned all his socks, and checked and rechecked his crossbow, and patrolled every night through the woodsmen's copse and around the boundary-stones of the village. He stood on the wood's edge and peered towards the little cluster of houses, the lights in the Fox and Feathers, the flags and garlands all up for the fair. They were as ready as they ever were. Wasn't every year Fabian took it into his head to go down to the pub in the first place; must have been five, six decades since he bothered with it last.

Tobias himself hadn't set foot in the Fox and Feathers since the night the stable boy—what was his name?—had run in gasping, straight from the Hall down the old woodland road, to say that the soldiers had come and that they'd already taken the others, Nathan, Simon, Thomas, the Jacks. There had been a terrible silence in the public house as the villagers had eyed Fabian sideways, fearing one of his explosions of temper. None of them would have called for the soldiers; they had more sense than to cross him. Tobias had half-stood. He still didn't know what he'd meant to do.

Then Fabian had put his hand on Tobias's sleeve.

"What's your hurry, Toby?" he'd said, and smiled his lovely smile. "One more round before we go."

He'd emptied his purse on the bar, and ordered the host to open a new cask; beer for the whole lot of them, every man in the village, and Fabian had sat back down and drunk his pint with lip-smacking enjoyment, eyes bright, his hand still on Tobias's sleeve. Then together they'd stood and walked out of the warm firelit room and into the breezy March night.

There was no moon, but the sky was washed with stars. Fabian whistled a tune as they walked into the woods: *and there to help the lady down was bloody-handed Toby.* Behind them in the distance Tobias heard the men, the hounds, the hunt.

"Nothing to worry about," Fabian said. "Not in Greenhallow." He smiled, his white teeth bright in the gloom. "Not in my wood."

Tobias walked beside him in petrified silence, while the hunters blundered and crashed in the undergrowth far behind, until they reached the old shrine.

"Ever seen the Wild Man, Toby?" Fabian said.

"Fairy stories," Tobias answered.

"Something like that," said Fabian, eyes bright and terrible, and he'd picked up a big white stone from near the shrine's base and weighed it in his hand.

Then he'd turned and smashed Tobias over the head with it. Tobias still remembered the feeling of his own temple crumpling, the split-second knowledge of his own end, and the darkness afterwards.

He'd woken at the foot of the old oak with time hanging heavy and green around him. He'd said Fabian's name, but there had been no one there. Not till the next spring did he finally meet the Lord of Summer, with his bright eyes, his lovely smile, his long red hair, and his company of dead men's souls. *Toby!* he'd cried.

Tobias had thought and thought about it, for four hundred years, until he'd reached the conclusion that Fabian must have loved him, after all, in his own way. That was the worst of it. The thing that woke now every year was always glad to see him. Tobias didn't know where he slept in between. The cavalcade of spectres that travelled with him had been mortal men themselves once, sure enough. What had Fabian found, woken, joined himself to in Greenhallow Wood? Something old, even older than the trees; something that should have been dead long ago.

Well. Another summer, and then he'd be gone again. And no need for him to ever clap eyes on Silver.

~

The day of the equinox dawned blustery and bright. Tobias saw sparks and shadows in the corners of his vision all the day long. Pearl refused to set foot outside his cottage all day; she curled on his bed and yowled at him whenever he came near. Bramble moved restlessly between the trees, trailing thorns wherever she went. Greenhallow waited.

And then near dusk Bramble lifted her head sharply and said, "Your fellow, your friend. He's here."

Tobias rolled his shoulders out and lifted his head slowly, and through the cloudy panes of his one good window he saw Henry Silver, good coat and mud-coloured curls and all, there in the midst of Tobias's wood on the very night Greenhallow's spectres would rise. "Damn him!" said Tobias. He jumped to his feet and rushed out.

"I hope you'll forgive me, Mr Finch," said Silver when he saw Tobias. "I know you weren't expecting to see me today, but the fact of the matter is that my mother has come to visit unexpectedly, and she has a number of opinions on the progress of my current research which ... well. I could do with the company of a friend. I brought a book, if you'd like me to read; or I could sing to you again, or ..."

He looked uncertain. There were heavy shadows under his eyes. Tobias stared at him. On this night of all nights, hiding from his mother: damn him, damn him. He couldn't go back to the Hall alone, and walking with him would be as good as shining a lantern on him. Tobias licked his lips and said, "You'd better stay here, then. You and Pearl can fight for the bed."

Silver's tired eyes lit up. "*Thank* you," he said. He pressed Tobias's hand as he passed him on the way into the cottage: too worn down to recall his manners, even. Tobias stood looking out into the dark under the trees for a moment, looking for movement, gleaming eyes, a flash of red. Nothing. Tobias took a deep breath and raised both his hands.

The trees crowded in close, leaving only a respectful space for the old oak; the path disappeared; mist descended thick beneath the branches. Bramble kicked up the earth—in the vegetable garden again, bless her—and dug her knotted toes into the soil, raising her thorns in earnest. Maybe the Lord of Summer would never know there'd been a mortal in his wood this night. Maybe he'd take his hungry ghosts and go down to the Fox and Feathers, up to the hills, out east to the boggy meadows there; they'd find some traveller, some beggar, some lost stranger, and that would be their prey for the season. Not Silver.

Tobias let his breath out in a long explosive sigh and turned and went into the cottage.

Fabian was already there.

"Evening, Toby," he said.

He was sitting on the floor by the fireplace, one long leg stretched out, his head tilted, wearing that friendly smile. Silver had taken Tobias's chair by the window. His good coat was hung over the back of it. You needed helping in and out of that coat, Tobias thought. Fabian must have done it, must have put his hands to Silver's shoulders and drawn it off and set it aside.

Silver's eyebrows were high. Fabian was dressed all in a grey that glimmered, and his old-fashioned cloak was pooling around him. His teeth were very white in his smiling face, a face that was almost lovelier now than it had been four hundred years ago when it had been lit by moonlight on the path down to the shrine. He spoke to Tobias but did not look at him: he was watching Silver with a steady, patient gaze. Pearl was crouched in the corner of the room with her tail lashing back and forth.

Something in Tobias's stomach twisted tight.

He'd known already this would happen. He'd known and hadn't let himself think of it. But whatever Tobias was, whatever he'd become when he woke under the old oak, was part of the Lord of Summer's domain.

"Who's this, Toby?" said Fabian. The glimmer was not

just his cloak: it was him as well. "I thought you hadn't any friends but me."

Tobias said nothing. Silver cast him an astonished gaze and then introduced himself politely.

"Silver," repeated Fabian caressingly. "What sort of a man are you, Silver?"

A bizarre question, plainly put. Silver stumbled and then said, "Well, a folklorist, I suppose. And an amateur—*very* amateur—archaeologist."

"I'm surprised you and Toby have anything to say to one another," said Fabian. "He's never thought much of fairy tales."

Silver blinked at that and visibly decided not to answer. "And you are?" he said instead.

Fabian's smile broadened, lovely, lazy, and he said, "I think you already know."

"Fabian," said Tobias.

"I heard you singing as I slept," Fabian said confidingly. "Sweet among the branches, under the old oak. I heard your voice calling my name, here in the Hallow, my domain. Silver singing in my wood; silver songs for summer's prince." Silver was blinking over and over, brow crumpling in a confused frown. "What a sweetmeat," Fabian said. "What a gift, Toby. My generous friend."

"Not this one," Tobias said. "No, Fabian, find another."

"Living in my *house*," said Fabian, and his eyes shone

bright, and his smile was fearsome. "No, Toby, I think it must be this one."

"I'm terribly sorry," mumbled Silver, "but did you say—I think you said—"

He trailed off.

Tobias said, "Fay, an you ever loved me."

Fabian stood up. He went and put his hand on the back of Silver's neck, proprietary, under the curls. It was more than Tobias had ever touched him. Silver got to his feet slowly. Tobias, not believing his own hand's daring, reached for the flint knife he kept at his belt. Fabian grinned.

The knife shattered in Tobias's grip.

"You may be Greenhallow's greatest servant, Toby," Fabian said, "but I am its master. Come, sweet." That to Silver, who followed him, stumbling a little, to the door, and then turned to Tobias and said slowly, "Mr Finch, could I ask—that is—"

He looked vaguely in the direction of his coat, still hanging on the back of Tobias's chair. "My notebook," he said.

"You shan't need it now," said Fabian softly, his mouth near Silver's ear.

"Of course not. Of course. If you could give it to my mother," said Silver. "Thank you. Yes . . . thank you. Good night."

"Good night, Toby," added Fabian, and he dropped his arm around Silver's shoulders as he steered him away. Shadows fell across his fair face as he turned away from the firelight, painting dark shapes across his brow, a bruise-hollow near his temple. Then he was gone. They both were gone.

Tobias pulled himself out of his stunned stillness and rushed out after them, but Fabian had vanished, of course. Of course. The trees were crowded close and the mist hung underneath them. Tobias could hear the sound of distant voices, stamping and shouting, the tinkling of bridle bells. He'd seen them only a few times over the centuries, but he heard them every year.

Bramble was there, but Tobias could not bring himself to speak. He went back inside and lay down on his old bed. Pearl never came and jumped up beside him. In the morning when he woke he found she'd curled herself on the chair with Silver's coat.

Tobias picked the coat up. He folded it carefully over his arm. He could feel the weight of Silver's little leather-bound notebook in an inner pocket. He thought of nothing. He set out for the Hall.

He did not try to step past the boundaries of the wood, but the young sapling that Bramble had made out of the walking stick Silver had given him months ago was still there, healthy and strong. Tobias carefully draped the coat over a low-hanging branch. Someone would find it, and Silver's notebook with it. That was all he could do.

At least there was no need to watch the village now, or patrol the borders, or do any of the things he normally did from March to September trying to keep Fabian well away from the world he no longer belonged to. With a handsome young playfellow to keep him amused Fabian was no threat to anyone for a season. That hadn't changed from the old days, when Fabian Rafela was master of Greenhallow Hall and Toby Finch was his faithful servant. Only what happened to the lad after was different now.

Tobias went back to his cottage and continued thinking of nothing.

II

Emily Tesh

"MR FINCH! MR FINCH! *MR FINCH*."

The voice had been calling for some time. Tobias did not look up from the flint he was working on. He needed another knife. The cottage could not be found as long as the wood kept it hidden.

"Mr Finch, I can stand here all day and I will," said the voice. Tobias looked up. Bramble, at the window, gave him a long questioning look: *Shall I?*

"And don't think you can send me off with thorns in my ears," added the voice tartly. "The very idea! I don't approve of you using a dryad for a guard dog, either. She's much too old to be running about this way; you'll go peculiar, young lady, if you keep this up."

"Who's there?" said Tobias, suddenly wary.

"Aha!" said the stranger. "I knew you must be around here somewhere. Come on out; let's have a look at you."

Tobias picked up his crossbow, loaded it, and went outside.

He recognised Silver's mother at once, though he'd never seen her before. She was shorter than he'd expected from Silver's description, and plumper. Her hair was scraped neatly back from her face, and greying, but it had the same muddy colour and loose wisps hung in the same curls. "Mr Finch," she said. "There will be no need for the crossbow. You *are* the Tobias Finch my son has been visiting regularly, yes?"

"The same," said Tobias.

She nodded, once. "And you are also, I believe, the individual known to local legend as *Bloody-Handed Toby*, a bandit and general good-for-nothing who haunted these environs some four hundred years ago as a member of Fabian Rafela's robber band." She brought up a hand and Tobias flinched, but all she was holding was Silver's little leather-bound notebook. "*And* you are, of course, the Wild Man of Greenhollow Wood. Or Green*hallow*, perhaps I should say. Henry's notes comment several times on your unusual pronunciation."

"Ma'am," began Tobias.

"Henry appears to have taken an embarrassingly long time reaching the obvious conclusions," said Silver's mother, "but then, he is rather new to this sort of thing. I am Mrs Adela Silver. You may call me Mrs Silver. And you, young lady?"

Bramble glowered suspiciously at her.

"I call her Bramble," said Tobias hoarsely.

"Bramble. Very good. Mr Finch," said Mrs Silver, "do put that crossbow down. You shall not need it in the immediate future. Let us sit down like civilised people, and then you will tell me what has happened to my son."

Tobias didn't move as she walked past him to the cottage door. "Mr *Finch*," she said in a voice like the snap of a whip, and he finally followed her in.

In the end he barely needed to speak. Mrs Silver seemed to know almost as much about his wood as he did. "Greenhollow has been a source of professional curiosity for some time," she said briskly, "but since it was plainly also being *managed*, quite adeptly, it was hardly a priority for investigation. Henry has always been more curious than practical, and although I attempted to dissuade him he could not resist the challenge. I take it you are in fact the manager." Her eyes flicked to his crossbow, his knives—flint and steel.

"You're another folklorist," said Tobias, trying to keep up.

"A *practical* folklorist," said Mrs Silver. "Vampires eliminated, ghouls laid to rest, fairies discouraged, and so on. It was my late husband's profession and now it is mine. And, in a small way, Henry's too, although he does not really have the stomach for some of the more hands-on elements. Now, I have read through his notes on Greenhollow and I believe I already know most of what is going on here, but there are some important pieces missing. Henry was convinced your Lord of Summer was some sort of fairy king and it seems to me he was on the wrong track entirely. The whole tangle here is plainly knotted up in the fate of the Rafela gang—five of whom were hanged, one of whom"—she nodded at Tobias—"is accounted for, and *one* of whom—"

"Fay took him," said Tobias. "Your son. Henry." He'd never used Silver's given name aloud before. It felt strange on his lips.

"*Took* him," said Mrs Silver, and her mouth went thin and her jaw tightened. "That answers one question. My other concerns the tree behind your little shack."

"The oak?" said Tobias.

"What is it?"

Tobias blinked at her. "The oak is the oak."

"According to my son's notes," said Mrs Silver, "that tree is the only thing in this wood apart from the old shrine which doesn't move. He noted that your cottage always appeared to be near it regardless of how else the landscape changed. Now, what *is* it, Mr Finch? A dryad of some description?"

"Him?" said Tobias. "No."

"Male dryads are uncommon but not unheard of—"

"No," said Tobias.

She subsided. "Well, I suppose the Wild Man should know," she said, slightly pettish. Then she sighed deeply and stood up. "A dryad would have been simpler. There's nothing else for it. The tree had better come down."

Tobias was on his feet before he'd made the decision. He stood grimly over her, knowing he was looming, trying to use his size to scare a human being for the first time in four centuries. Mrs Silver looked up at him with pale, sharp eyes that were, Tobias thought, remarkably like her son's. She did not sound the least bit kind as she said, "I am afraid you will not be able to prevent this. The wood is Henry's property, and I have his power of attorney."

"The wood is *mine*," said Tobias.

"No, I don't believe it is. Not by any measure."

"You—"

"Mr Finch," said Mrs Silver, "you have told me that my son has been taken by your Lord of Summer, who is some species of spectre or possibly an unusual type of higher revenant; not a vampire but not dissimilar. Do you know where he is?"

Tobias said nothing.

"Do you believe you can find him? Do you believe you can save him? Do you have any ability to command, control, or otherwise *manage* Fabian Rafela?"

"I'm bound up in that tree, woman," said Tobias abruptly. He'd never said it before. "Do you mean to murder me?"

She regarded him coolly. "Mr Finch, if I understand the situation correctly, you have already outlived your proper lifespan by some four hundred years," she said. "My son is twenty-three."

Tobias's hands were shaking. He could not speak.

"I will do this with your cooperation or without it," said Mrs Silver. "But if the old oak is Greenhollow's heart, then Rafela is as bound to it as you are. It must come down."

"He's likely dead already," said Tobias, feeling his insides as hollow and rotten-soft as any dying thing.

Mrs Silver raised her eyebrows. "The Lord of Summer rides from March till September," she said. "I doubt he has finished with Henry yet."

There was a long silence as they looked at each other.

"You'll want Charlie Bondee," said Tobias at last. "Ask in the village. He's a decent shot as well as a good woodsman. Might be needful."

"I shall be back tomorrow," said Mrs Silver.

~

Tobias was up before the sun, but Mrs Silver didn't appear until noon. He spent the morning finishing the edge on his new flint knife. Then he fetched his axe from the woodblock and sharpened it, sitting on his doorstep with his bare feet in the earth. Bramble paced worriedly around and around the cottage. Pearl watched her with her tail lashing. Tobias kept his eyes down, watching the flick of Pearl's tail, the tangled thorns of Bramble's movement, his own big square fingers on the axe handle across his knees. If he looked up, he would see the old oak with his spreading branches.

Mrs Silver turned up when the sun was at its height, with Charlie Bondee in tow. The boy had his pistol, and more to the point he had his own axe and a big two-man saw which he was carrying across his back. Tobias stood up when he saw them coming. Bondee looked at him, and for a moment Tobias imagined seeing himself through the lad's eyes: tall and broad, with heavy shoulders and big hands, long wild hair and bare feet planted in the ground—and here was Bramble curling around him, standing by him, not bothering to conceal herself from human eyes now, so that Tobias was wrapped in thorns and crowned with leaves: the Wild Man of Greenhollow, a lunatic, a bandit, a follower of the old gods, or at least of something like them. Bondee looked afraid. Of course he did. In all of four hundred years, only Silver had never been afraid.

"Pay no attention to him," said Mrs Silver. "Or the dryad. It's not *her* tree."

Well, thought Tobias, Silver and his mother.

Bondee swallowed a few times. Then he looked up at the old oak. His expression went doubtful.

"It's a big job," he said. "A job and a half. Be faster with more men."

"I very much doubt that a large group could even find the place," said Mrs Silver. "Two will have to do. You shan't interfere, Mr Finch." She said it as a fact, not a request: Tobias would not come between her and her hunt for her son. She barely even looked at him.

Bondee blinked at her as he took in what she meant by *two*. "Ma'am, it's not ladies' work."

"You are not the first man to say that to me," said Mrs Silver.

"But—"

"You'll never handle that saw, Mrs Silver," said Tobias quietly. He was still holding his axe. He came and stood by Bondee, and made himself look up at the oak. "We'll need rope," he said to the woodsman.

"Aye," said Bondee after a moment in which Tobias pretended he hadn't seen the young man's hand twitch towards his pistol.

"I've enough," said Tobias. "Mrs Silver." He nodded at her. She looked at him for a long moment, familiar pale eyes fixed on Tobias's own, and then she went to fetch the rope.

~

It took hours to bring the tree down.

He was too big for easy felling, bigger by far than the slender many-trunked lovelies of the copse that the woodsmen tended year upon year. He'd been a mighty old king of the forest before Tobias ever came near Greenhallow. Bondee had a queer kind of admiration for him. "Must be eight hundred years on him, easy," he said.

"More than that," said Tobias. Maybe not the full three thousand years back to Silver's primaeval forest—what had he called it—the Hallow Wood. But the time of the wood ran deepest here beneath the oak: maybe so, then.

They used rope, and they had Mrs Silver hold the ladder, and they went up into the crown of the old oak's branches to lop him back a piece at a time. Each of the thick branches they brought down would have made a whole trunk for a lesser tree. Bondee kept shaking his head in astonishment. "Fine timber, as well," he said.

"It shall have to be burnt," said Mrs Silver. "Just in case." She had a queer focus in her eyes as she watched them work, and she was constantly moving, watching and calling out and offering to fetch and carry and lift things, all with the energy of a much younger woman. Bramble had disappeared somewhere. Tobias didn't blame her for not wanting to watch this. It was a cruel thing to do to a fine old tree.

By evening nothing was left of the oak's spreading

leafy crown. Tobias stood back on the ground and looked up at the crooked shape of the naked trunk, each curving gesture at a branch coming to an abrupt and ugly halt. A full moon floated beyond it, and the tree's wreckage cast silvered shadows all around. "Right," said Bondee. "We'll have him down tomorrow."

"Mr Bondee, if you attempt to walk home through the wood with the job undone, I assure you that you will be dead well before morning," said Mrs Silver. "We will certainly have the full attention of Greenhollow and its preternatural inhabitants by now. The tree must fall by midnight."

~

It took a long time, with Tobias and Bondee both working the big saw, to bring the great trunk down. Mrs Silver sat on a felled branch with Pearl, the traitress, purring in her lap, and stroked her absently left-handed as she watched. She had a small pistol of her own, pearl-handled, close by her right hand. Silver bullets, Tobias guessed. He'd never made any use of silver. Had to make do with flint.

"Wait!" said Bondee when they were near enough to done, and Tobias wiped sweat off his brow and stood up. Bondee was squinting in the moonlight. Mist had come up out of the trees around them. Tobias looked around and saw that the shape of things had moved while they worked. The wood did that plenty, but it seldom did it to him.

"That can't be right," said Bondee, looking from the oak to Tobias's cottage and then back to the oak. They'd started the work angling so the tree would fall away. Now after the forest's shifting the great trunk would come down right through Tobias's roof.

Tobias looked at the tree. He thought of four hundred years repairing and re-repairing that roof; of scrubbing out the floors, fixing the doors and shutters, planting and replanting his little garden. Four hundred years while his cottage grew around him like a tree growing its rings; Pearl's mother and grandmother and great-great-great-great-grandmother all the way back to the cat who'd ambled around Greenhallow Hall when Fabian had been its master; four hundred years of the wood, and barely a soul passing through the whole time. Bramble had never set foot in the cottage, nor had any of her sisters. No fairy would ever have come near the place. And of mortals a few, a very few, and of all those only Henry Silver more than once.

And he thought of Henry Silver: soaking wet the first time Tobias saw him, wringing out his hair and smiling, trying to flirt the whole damn time—trying though he must have known damn well what Tobias was, after all, all that time while his pale eyes were watching; must have been keeping *notes* in his damn *notebook* about it. Silver sitting with him when he had that hole in his leg, after paying for a doctor, telling him old stories; Silver among his books, turning his face up from the map he'd drawn; Silver's voice rolling up and down, full of hills and valleys, Silver blushing rosy pink when he sang.

Henry Silver, here in Tobias's wood, human as could be, until the moment Fabian decided to take him away.

Bondee was suggesting ways they could get around the problem of the old oak's fall. Tobias shook his head to all of them. "There's nothing that'll stop him coming down where he wants," he said. "Let it happen." He looked again at his cottage, neat and tidy as it was. There were things in it that he might have tried to save, if he thought he was going to survive all this. But Mrs Silver was right: he'd outlived his right to be in the world long ago. Time to have done, then.

Bondee looked at him nervously but didn't dare argue. They finished the felling. The great trunk came down in the end with a crash, down through Tobias's roof and all the tidy rings of his long existence. The neat little cottage was a smashed ruin. Whatever came out of this night, Tobias knew he would never live there again.

Now there was nothing in the clearing but wreckage

and the gigantic stump. Mrs Silver was on her feet with her pistol in her hand. The mist was boiling out of the trees around them now, and the whole wood thrummed with the expectation of *something*. Tobias, remembering the sounds of jingling bits and horses' hooves, picked up his crossbow. Whatever it was that Fabian belonged to now, there were a lot of them. Scores more in the last four hundred years; Tobias had cause to know.

He heard the hooves, and the bridle bells. But nothing came out of the mist. Mrs Silver lifted her chin and peered around. "It must be now," she said—firmly, but Tobias could hear the worry underneath. She wanted her son, of course. "With the tree dead it *must* be—"

"Tree's not dead," said Tobias, before Bondee could.

He knew it the same way the woodsman knew it, because he knew trees: but he also knew it with the knowledge of the Wild Man of Greenhallow, who felt every slow green beat of the forest's heart. You could cut a tree down to nothing and it'd still put out shoots in the springtime, if the roots went deep enough. The forest would feed it, the sun would wake it. And no roots were deeper than the old oak's.

"We haven't the tools for the stump," said Bondee. He was holding his gun too. Tobias hoped Mrs Silver had shared her silver bullets. "We'll need horse and chain for that, or else gunpowder, for the size of it." He sounded afraid: spooked, no doubt, by the mist and the bells.

"It *must* be done by morning!" snapped Mrs Silver.

"It's not possible, ma'am—"

Tobias said, "I'll do it."

Bondee stared at him. Mrs Silver's pale eyes fixed on him too. She didn't look confused like the lad did. Tobias nodded at her. After a moment she returned the nod, regally, and held up a hand to cut Bondee off when he started to object.

Tobias turned to the great stump, wide across as a dining table.

"Out you come, now," he murmured. He planted his feet a shoulders width apart in the ground. After a moment he closed his eyes.

Here was the wood.

Slow and green he felt the life of it, the life that had been his life as well these four centuries past. It poured around him thick and steady, binding all together: the long patient strength of the trees that anchored, the deep bright power of the handful of dryads—Tobias felt Bramble clear as day among them, young and strong—and then the small and necessary, the bracken and ferns, the mosses and mushrooms. Here were the songbirds and ravens and solemn wide-winged owls, shy deer and burrowing rabbits, fox and badger and snake, beetles and moths and midges, all the things that were the wood, that lived each in their own way under the shelter of the old oak.

And here was the oak, no more dead than Tobias was, living in all he had shaped and was a part of. Here was the great stump that was the least of him. And here—

Tobias felt his footing shift as something crumbled beneath him, and he fell to his knees, almost choking on a sudden gust of foul air that seemed to come out of nowhere. This was not rot. Rot belonged in the wood; it fed the must, went back to the soil, brought forth mushrooms in the wet dark. This was different. It was a foulness that refused to surrender to cleansing decay. Year on year it endured, throwing off poison in all directions, waiting in the dark, coiling itself into the fabric of the wood. He grunted with the effort of keeping it from dragging him in. The stump, he thought, though he could barely think of why any longer, and Silver and Silver's mother and the poor woodsman were all a fleeting dream. Time to uproot the stump.

The roots moved in the earth like mighty snakes. Soil rattled away from them. Things knotted deep in the ground cracked and groaned. Bondee let out a stifled oath. Mrs Silver stood up straight. Tobias heard himself let out a wordless roar, and the stump heaved itself from the shuddering ground.

It was a long time before Tobias could lever himself

upright again. When he stood up at last and his swimming vision settled, he saw that Bondee had fainted dead away. Mrs Silver was watching Tobias with a curious look. The stump and its coils of broken roots lay uprooted among the wreckage of the oak in the clearing. The moon-silvered mist was thicker than ever all around them. And where the oak had stood there was a great dark hollow in the ground, gaping open like a mouth. Tobias could still taste foulness in the air, bubbling up from below.

"No wonder Henry was fascinated," said Mrs Silver softly, still looking at Tobias. "You are a marvel of the unnatural, Mr Finch."

Tobias grunted.

"Well, then," she said, turning her attention to the hollow. "Let us descend."

Tobias could think of nothing he wanted to do less than to walk down into that darkness. But Mrs Silver came to his side and held out her arm, imperious. "I am not as sprightly as I once was," she said. "I would appreciate your assistance on the slope."

They went down together. The earth underfoot heaved with crawling things fleeing back into the safety of the upturned soil. Every step forward made Tobias's mouth taste sourer. Silver's mother seemed fearless, but her hand on Tobias's forearm gripped very tightly. The hollow itself was not deep: it seemed to be nothing more or less than the space carved out by the old oak's growing. Cracked tangles of roots still poked roughly out of the walls.

"I hope they passed Bondee by," murmured Mrs Silver after a moment.

Tobias looked up and saw what she meant: the mist that had lurked around the clearing had boiled in closer and now hung over the hollow. He could no longer make out the stars in the sky. It was not dark, but he knew the light they walked by was no longer moonlight.

Mrs Silver tripped. "Careful, now," Tobias said.

"I shouldn't have looked down," she replied, and for the first time she sounded shaken.

Tobias glanced down and then made himself carefully look up again.

They were walking through a scattered pile of bones. Even a moment's look had been enough to know that there were many bodies here: scores, hundreds. Horse skulls were strewn among the human bones here and there. There had been a graveyard beneath the oak, buried deep, deeper every year, feeding on the wood as the wood fed upon it in turn.

At the heart of the pit there was a stone, pitted with time, carved in long grooves. Tobias had never seen it before. He could feel the cold age of it, older than the shrine by the village, older than the barrows on the hills.

"That, I suppose, is an altar," said Mrs Silver, with an admirable pretence of calm.

"Aye. For the old gods," Tobias said.

Two figures lay on the ancient stone. One was nothing more than papery grey skin stretched over old bones. Its clothes were rotten rags, and the shape of its teeth was plainly visible under the desiccated flesh of its face. There was a dent in its temple, as if something had broken the skull there. Its hair lay coiled in a brittle braid along its back, still faintly reddish in colour.

Wrapped in its arms, gripped by bony fingers tipped with long yellow nails, was Henry Silver.

He lay there as if pleasantly sleeping; his mouth was curved in a faint smile. His mud-coloured curls fell loose around his face, and his collar and cuffs were undone. He'd taken his boots off before he lay down, Tobias saw: they sat neatly side by side at the foot of the altar. Mrs Silver squared her shoulders and marched to his side. She hooked her hands under his arms to pull him from the corpse's embrace and drag him from the altar. Tobias could have helped her. Silver was a big weight for a little woman to manage and would have been no trouble at all for him. He could have helped, but he was watching Fabian.

In another lifetime perhaps he would have been the

one to dash forward and pull someone he loved away from this ancient and ugly sorcery. Perhaps. Fabian's dry body did not try to keep hold of Silver. It did not move at all. Tobias kept looking at the dent in its temple and remembering over and over the shadow-bruise on Fabian's face the night he had taken Silver away, and the sensation of his own skull crumpling on that long-ago evening when Fabian picked up a white stone and smashed Tobias's head with it.

"Mother?" he heard Silver say, groggily, and then, "Mr Finch?"

"Henry, honestly, how *could* you be such a fool," said Mrs Silver.

"*Mother,*" said Silver, protesting.

Tobias was watching Fabian's corpse. He watched its eyes open and its bony hands flex. The flint knife felt cool and steady when his fingers wrapped around it. He walked across the bone-strewn floor and stood over the cracked altar. The dead man looked up at him silently. Four hundred years, bound to the wood, waiting every summer for Fabian to rise out of the shadows blazing like the sun.

Tobias looked at him a little longer. Silver came up beside him and put a hand on his shoulder. "Come away, Mr Finch," he said, low and sweet.

Tobias turned with flint in hand and stabbed him through the eye.

Mrs Silver screamed shrilly. Tobias heard a shot and felt bright pain bloom in his shoulder from one of her silver bullets. Silver staggered backwards with the knife sticking out of his skull, and then he began to laugh.

"Toby," he said, "oh, Toby, Toby, Toby, you were always cleverer than you looked."

"Damn you, Fay," said Tobias, holding his wounded shoulder.

"I was going to seduce you so prettily," said Fabian, grinning at him out of Silver's face with blood dripping from his eye socket. "I was going to sing you songs. We'd do everything all over again, right from the start."

"*Fuck* you."

"An you ever loved me," mocked Fabian. "Toby, I *always* loved you." He held his arms stretched out wide. "We'll bring the wood right up to the house again. We'll swallow it whole. We'll sleep in feather beds. You can chase off every monster but me. What do you say, Toby?"

"You're a dead man, Fay," said Tobias, "and even when you were alive you were wicked right through."

"Not *right* through," said Fabian. "Not right through, Toby; be fairer than that." He reached up and plucked the knife out of his eye. Blood flooded down the side of his face, and then it slowed to a trickle, and then the trickle turned to dust. He turned and grinned at Mrs Silver. "Oh,

Mother, Mother," he said. "Do you know, I don't remember ever having a mother."

"Henry," she said. Her voice shook.

"Not I," said Fabian. "I am the Lord of Summer, the Master of the Hallow, the prince-by-corpselight. I was here before your darling Henry bought my house; in fact," he laughed, "I was here before Fabian Rafela's grandfather *built* my house."

The corpse on the altar was still trying to move, twitching its bone fingers, blinking its dull eyes. Tobias was bleeding. "Fay," he said.

"You thought you could take him from me? You thought you could cut down a tree and that would be enough? This is my wood," said Fabian. "Nothing happens here except by my leave. I *am* Greenhall—"

He let out a piercing screech that did not sound human, and stumbled. Thorny vines had burst from the ground and were snatching at his bare feet. Fabian kicked and swore at them. Tobias blinked, and then blinked again, and suddenly time was pouring slow and green around him, and in its slowness and greenness five tall figures were in the hollow.

He only recognised the smallest of them. The others he had never seen apart from their trees. Bramble's eyes were glowing like a cat's in the shadows. She was summoning thorn bushes and nettles by the score to tear at the ghoulish thing that was Fabian's mind and Silver's body and the soul of something that Tobias could tell was older by far than both, near as old as the wood: a parasite that had bored in deep long ago.

Tobias wanted to cry out and tell Bramble that it was a waste of time to try to kill the thing that way. All she would do was get herself uprooted for good. But then he realised that she was doing nothing of the sort. While Fabian struggled and swore at her, the other four dryads had taken themselves to the ancient altar and the dry body that lay there.

In the slow green that was the time of the wood Tobias saw them set about the stone. They planted themselves one at each corner, four tall slender aspen trees, and their roots went plunging down into the earth like long spears plunged into flesh. The bones of men and horses that carpeted the hollow cracked and scattered as the new trees grew and grew.

In a matter of moments the altar stone broke. The papery corpse that Fabian had shed like a snakeskin fell to earth. Time suddenly dashed forward like a flooding stream again. Tobias made for the broken stone, reaching out for the body, thinking of the panicked intelligence in those dim eyes. He saw the roots turn it over and push it down, forcing it into earth, more compost. There was a scent in the air of good clean rot as the wood took hold of the hollow.

Fabian screamed in Silver's voice when the altar cracked. He howled words in a language Tobias did not know, and the spectres that Tobias had heard every year in the mist flooded down the slope towards them all, bringing their light that was not moonlight with them. But the dryads forced their bones under the ground, splitting them smaller and smaller, and the ghosts of all the murdered youths who'd lain on the altar dissipated before they reached the bottom of the pit. Fabian snarled at last and turned on Bramble, who tried in vain to tangle him in thorny vines. He gripped them and they turned grey and then white and fell apart in his grasp. He spat another word in that strange tongue and Tobias cried out hoarsely as Bramble fell, curling in on herself, already cracked and browning at her edges. Fabian looked up at him with Silver's pale eyes and gave him a sweetly furious smile as he lifted his hands over the crumpling dryad.

A shot rang out in the hollow.

A hole appeared in Fabian's forehead. He lifted slow hands as if shocked. Blood poured from the wound, and then dust. The dust kept coming. Tobias said, "Fay!" before he meant to, as Fabian stared and stumbled and then collapsed. He was turning to dust even as he fell, Silver's body blowing away in the fine midnight breeze that was suddenly sighing through the hollow, shaking the four tall new aspen trees. The breeze kissed the sweat that was dripping down Tobias's forehead and turned him chill and clammy. It tugged at the curls that were falling out of Mrs Silver's neat hairstyle as she lowered her little pearl-handled pistol.

~

They shook Bondee awake and went back to the Hall.

Tobias felt nothing when he crossed the boundary of the wood. He helped Mrs Silver up the stairs and delivered her into the hands of a confused maidservant who took her away, but not before she had ordered that they both be given rooms for the night. The housekeeper knew Bondee—he was her nephew or some such; all Silver's staff were locals—but looked askance at Tobias, plainly not pleased to see him again. Tobias said nothing. Someone brought him bandages and he took care of the wound in his shoulder, painful but shallow. Then he had nowhere to go, so he went to the bedroom where Silver had put him to convalesce, the room with white walls and heavy furniture where he had first read Tobias the tales he chased like butterflies.

Tobias sat down on the clean white bed and put his head in his hands and sobbed like a child. The sun was rising before he finally slept.

~

And there was April, and there was May; spring painting the land with tender green, summer swelling fruit on the bough. Tobias did not feel it. Tobias stayed in the white room, slept like a log on the heavy bed, and said nothing to anyone. Twice a day a servant brought him food on a tray. Mrs Silver must have ordered it. Tobias ate the food, but he would not have missed it if it had not been there.

Mrs Silver came to him after a time. She asked sharp little questions, about Fay, about the wood. Tobias answered them because it seemed the easiest way to have her to leave him be. She'd been into the library, into Silver's books. She'd found Fay's books there too. Silver had had them all along, bought them off obscure collectors, dug them out of old libraries: pieces of Fabian Rafela's life as scoundrel and scholar and halfway wizard. Tobias felt nothing about it. He felt nothing about anything. Mrs Silver brought him one and pointed at a page, the sizzling loops of Fay's handwriting under a diagram and Silver's notes around it. Tobias told her he couldn't read, said nothing else, and endured her scorn and frustration as he might have endured a passing rainstorm.

Mrs Silver couldn't find the place where the cottage had been, the grave of the old oak. It hadn't occurred to Tobias she'd try. She wanted Silver, he saw eventually.

Twenty-three years old. Of course she wanted Silver.

She'd get nothing back of her son now. The wood had taken him. Tobias had seen it happen.

Then on the first of June Mrs Silver received a letter from a woman who wrote about a cursed lake that took children every year. She summoned Tobias to her study and read it aloud to him.

"Nixie," said Tobias, eventually, when it became clear that Mrs Silver was waiting for him to say something. "Young 'un."

"You're certain?"

"Had one in the old pond a few years back."

"When?" said Mrs Silver.

Tobias thought hard. "Forty-six. No, forty-four."

"Which century?"

Tobias shrugged.

Mrs Silver sighed. "Well."

Tobias said nothing.

"Maybe the change of seasons matters to Greenhollow," she said. "Maybe it must be the equinox before I can find him."

Nothing.

"A nixie," she said. "I've never encountered one before. You had better accompany me."

She took Tobias to town.

They travelled on the stagecoach, then a hundred and

twenty miles west by train. The train was a belching smoking monster of a thing. The people looked warily at Tobias's tall figure and long hair, but when he picked up Mrs Silver's luggage for her they stopped seeing him. The nixie wasn't so much trouble, in the end, though Tobias got soaked head to toe and caught a cold after. He sneezed glumly on the train all the way back to town, and there they found three more letters waiting for Mrs Silver, each more urgent than the last.

There were more letters after that, and after that. Mrs Silver gave Tobias a permanent room in the townhouse and a wage. "My assistant," she said to the few who asked. Tobias felt the absence of the wood as an itch in his heart, but there was nothing real to it. He didn't belong to the wood anymore, nor it to him.

The town was full of tall smoke-stained buildings, with glass windows that were not cloudy and flawed. It was never dark from night to morning: gas lamps burned in the streets all night long, and Tobias never saw the stars. It was as unlike Greenhallow as it could possibly be. At first it was a nothing of a place, but the months went by, and the room in the townhouse became familiar. It was not the cottage that he had kept precisely to his liking, but it was clean and dry and warm. He spent his wages on baubles at the market, odd little things that took his fancy, porcelain-faced statuettes and prints on card of sailing ships and coloured glass bottles. They were the things of this world and of this time, human right through. Tobias started to find he liked them.

He kept his flint knife and his steel, his crossbow, a new pistol loaded with plain lead bullets and a little pouch of silver shot he wore at his belt. He laid monsters low across wide swathes of country he'd never seen before; even a few in the towns, turned nastier by their confusion. Sometimes the letters requested Mr Finch and Madam Silver both.

The world was far bigger than Tobias remembered from four centuries ago. It was bigger than he had ever known, and he was living in it. He had thought himself a thing uprooted, like the great oak, ready to begin his death.

"Mr Finch," said Mrs Silver, the one time he said anything about it, "you are not, in point of fact, a tree."

Summer, autumn. Long, cold winter days which Mrs Silver spent with her books while Tobias tramped around town, peering into shop windows, watching the people hurry along the cobbled streets. Occasionally he got accosted by thieves; he only looked at them and they went away. Once a group of small children followed him down the street, hooting and throwing stones that landed safely shy of his new leather boots. It was a far cry from getting shot by Charlie Bondee when he saw the wild man come out of the wood.

Mrs Silver never made Tobias cut his hair, but she sniffed when she looked at him occasionally. Eventually, he plucked up his courage and trimmed it himself, taking the worst of rattiness off the ends. The hanks of hair that fell away from the scissors never turned to dead grass and scattered bark. They stayed as scruffy knots of human hair. Tobias was not now what he had been before.

January. February. Tobias felt time as a physical thing dragging him along. On the first of March, Mrs Silver booked a hire coach to take them back to Greenhollow Hall. She didn't say a word about it to Tobias until the night before. He found himself unsurprised.

She'd never held a funeral for Henry, never wept a tear. When her acquaintances asked her about her son, she told them nothing at all. Tobias still saw in his dreams more often than he'd like the solid young body with Fabian's mad light in its pale eyes blowing away like dust; he saw the withered corpse getting ploughed under the earth by the roots of the aspen trees.

They spent the first three weeks of March at the Hall on the edge of the wood. Tobias never set foot in it, and he doubted Mrs Silver did either. Locals came by to pay her their respects. Tobias kept to the white room that he thought of by now as his. When memories of Silver pushed themselves forward for his attention he got out

Emily Tesh

his knives and sharpened them one by one. When he'd run out of knives to sharpen he started darning all his socks. He'd put plenty of holes in them over the last year.

The sun rose on the day of the equinox, and Mrs Silver went to the wood. Tobias watched her go and did not follow.

She came back after dusk, dry-eyed, and came to his room. "Mr Finch," she said.

"Ma'am," said Tobias.

She looked at him for a long time. She was a fearsome woman, but Tobias's vision doubled, and he saw someone tired, getting older, with no family in the world but one lost son. Fabian hadn't remembered ever having a mother. Tobias remembered his, vaguely, but he could not have told the colour of her hair, or the sound of her voice.

"I do not blame myself," she said. "Henry and I disagreed that night, but he knew when he invited me to inspect the progress of his research that we were likely to disagree. In any case, by the time I reached that altar it was already too late."

"If there's a fault, Mrs Silver," said Tobias, "it's mine."

He had not said it aloud before. But it was the truth.

Mrs Silver snorted. "On the contrary. You specifically told Henry *not* to visit you on the equinox. If I know my son—"

She halted.

"I imagine he planned to argue with me that night," she went on thinly after a moment. "Precisely to give himself an excuse, you understand. Nothing, Mr Finch, has ever stopped Henry from pursuing his own curiosity to the uttermost limits of folly."

Tobias said nothing. It was not Silver he was thinking of now. It was Fay in his library, as it had been before the big windows and mahogany shelves: maybe two dozen books, and the young master of the Hall with his red braid and his brilliant smile and the secrets of the old gods held in the hollow of his hand. Fay seeking riches, and beauty, and immortality.

Silver at least had never had any cruelty in him.

"Aye," he managed at last. There was nothing else to say.

"I believe," said Mrs Silver, "that you know Greenhollow Wood better than anyone."

Tobias said nothing.

"His body for burial, at least," she said. "Tell your dryads that. They do not need his bones." Her jaw stiffened. "And I do."

Tobias stood up slowly, took up all his sharpened knives one by one, and his crossbow, and the new pistol.

Alone by moonlight he went out to the wood.

~

Near the threshold he passed a strong young sapling with an oddly knotted trunk. No one would ever have taken it for a former walking stick. Tobias placed his hand on the bark a moment, but it was only a tree. If he had not known better, he would have thought it no different from any other young tree in the wood.

He kept moving, listening to his footfalls in the damp mulch, smelling the wet spring scent of growth. There were fronded ferns putting out fans of fresh green along the gully of the stream, and rotting autumn leaves still heaped by the wind in some of the clearings. The blue-bells were putting up their early sharp stems like soldiers; no flowers till April, but there were patches of crocus here and there promising future colour.

Tobias walked nearly two hours and never saw a sign of the clearing where his cottage had been. No flicker in the corner of his vision gave away Bramble with her sunlit eyes. Nothing uncanny moved in the branches: no corpselight mists roiled beneath the canopy. He heard night-calling insects, and the rattling sigh of the wind in the leaves, and once the distant high-pitched screech of a fox.

At last he knew he was beaten. He sat on a mossy stump and closed his eyes. Not even Silver's bones for his mother; not even that. Well, what did the wood care for mothers? Tobias should have known.

Then he heard a chirrup. A warm head butted itself under his hand.

Tobias opened his eyes. It was Pearl, looking healthy and pleased with herself, tabby coat dappled in the moonlight. She leapt into Tobias's lap and stretched, pricking his legs with her claws as she unsheathed them, for all the world as if he had not been gone an hour, let alone a year. Tobias found his mouth making an uncertain shape that was nearly a smile. He scratched the cat's ears, which she seemed to accept as her due.

He did not know how long he sat on the stump, there in the dark with the cat on his knee and the sounds of the wood around him. At last she jumped down and trotted away into the shadows and he stood up. There was a pinkish quality to the dimness which meant that dawn would come soon. He doubted Mrs Silver had slept. He would have to return to the Hall and tell her the truth: that he had found nothing, that there would never be anything to find. He sighed.

"She never sits so long with me," said a voice among the trees.

Tobias looked up sharply. His hand went at once towards a knife.

Silver was there in the shadow of the trees. His pale

eyes gleamed in the dim light. His hair was curling loose around his face. He was smiling.

"What," said Tobias, in a voice like the croak of a raven, and he swallowed and tried again. His heart was hammering in his chest. "What—"

Silver's smile fell off his face and he ran forward as Tobias half-sat, half-fell back onto the stump with his breath coming in sharp wheezes. Four hundred years he had never had to worry about his body giving out on him. Silver seized his hands and said, "Mr Finch—Mr Finch—*Tobias*—"

Tobias concentrated on keeping his breathing even as Silver spoke frantically to him. "I'm so very sorry—I had no idea it would be such a shock—Tobias, please—"

When Tobias could finally see straight again, he saw that Silver was kneeling in front of him and looking very ashamed of himself. He was still holding on to both of Tobias's hands. "Are you well?" he said. "I *am* sorry."

"You *rat*," said Tobias.

"I didn't expect that to happen," said Silver. "You always seemed so immovable—like a boulder, a mountain—I thought you might raise your brows at me, at the most."

"How long?" said Tobias.

Silver didn't pretend to misunderstand. "I woke up at midwinter. It was dark. Midnight exactly, I expect, though the ladies are rather vague on concepts like celestial mechanics, and they only rustle at me if I ask them about it."

"What are you?" said Tobias.

Silver smiled at him. He lifted both hands and ran them through his mud-coloured hair, and then he held them out to Tobias.

Tobias saw the green stains on his fingers. He could not speak.

"I'm more or less what you were, I think," said Silver. "Though—I had no idea, I really didn't. Tobias, how did you do it? How on earth did you stay so human? I keep trying, but the *time*—it just falls away from me. I tried to mend your cottage." Tobias snorted. "I know, I know, but the wood seemed willing to help, so I did my best, but I kept getting distracted and going for a walk, as it seemed to me for an hour or two, and I'd come back and find everything I'd built undone and ivy growing everywhere. Don't laugh at me!"

Tobias tried to stop. There was a smile that wanted to creep onto his face no matter what. "Took me a fair while to get the hang of it," he said. "You don't have to live by the wood's count the whole time. Better not. Keep a cat, or something like it, and it'll keep you awake."

"Pearl seems to look after herself," said Silver. "I tried to take care of her for you—"

Tobias shook his head. "She does as she pleases. Never mind it."

"Tobias—Mr Finch, that is," said Silver, and then he smiled an irrepressible, dimpled smile and said, "In fact, no, *Tobias*. It's so good to see you. I missed you. The wood missed you."

"I don't belong here now," Tobias said.

"You belong at least as much as the Hall and the village and the woodsmen. Didn't you tell me that people were a piece of Greenhollow as well?" Silver frowned. "Unless—it might have been the wood which told me that. Sometimes it seems to me that it speaks with your voice still. Four hundred years, you know, is a decent length of time even for a tree. Yes, we missed you. Where did you go? Where have you been?"

Tobias told him.

He told him about the nixie, and the ghoul pack, and the spectral hound he'd shot on a moor a hundred miles north. He told him about the town, and the children who'd followed him through the streets, and the rattling stinking speed of the steam trains all over the country. Silver listened smiling, cross-legged on the moss now at Tobias's feet, and Tobias talked himself hoarse, talking of the year he'd had while Silver slept beneath the wood.

"And you'd better come to see your mother," he concluded after all was said, "and beg her pardon."

Silver shuddered theatrically. "Must I?"

"None of that," said Tobias sharply. "She's a nice lady and you've given her a nasty scare."

There was a pause.

"My God," said Silver, "you like my mother."

Tobias frowned at him.

"But of course you like my mother; she's nearly as prickly as Bramble. Does *she* like *you*?" Silver peered at him. "She does! Heaven help me, I've made a terrible mistake."

"What do you mean?" said Tobias.

"Only that I never attempt to make myself charming to men my mother likes," said Silver. "She knows my habits and she's always run my life for me. The Greenhollow investigation was the first thing I'd ever done without her peering over my shoulder the whole time." He grinned. "And—don't say it—I got myself captured by some revenant perversion of the old gods and buried alive by a gang of dryads and now I'm bound to a wood. Really I think it went quite well, don't you? But my point is—I forget what my point was."

"That you don't get friendly with men your mother likes," said Tobias.

"Well," said Silver, smiling up at him, "not as a general rule. For you, my dear fellow, I think I can make an exception."

"You're a damned flirt as well as a rat," Tobias said bluntly.

Silver laughed, a bright peal in the quiet air. Dappled dawn light was drawing pictures in the leafy shadows that fell across him from above. "You've changed," he said. "It suits you."

Tobias shrugged.

"At this rate maybe I really *will* manage to charm you someday. I've been trying for so long. Since we first met in that rainstorm, do you recall? You helped me take my coat off, and I had cold water dripping down the back of my neck, and I was sure the moment I saw you that I'd found the Wild Man of Greenhollow. It seemed like the luckiest stroke of my life."

Tobias stood up. He reached down a hand and pulled Silver to his feet. Silver wasn't expecting it and stumbled a little. He felt heavier to Tobias than he should have been; there was a weight and solidity to him now that went beyond the physical, that had deep roots. Tobias paid it no mind. He put his big hand round the back of Silver's head, into his mud-coloured curls, and kissed him.

Silver's lips parted in surprise underneath his. It only lasted an instant, and then Tobias let him go.

"I'm charmed," he said gruffly. "Come beg your mother's pardon."

Silver followed him, looking rather shocked. He started to speak a time or two but trailed off. "I'm not sure I can leave the wood," he said, when the trees were thinning and the Hall was in sight.

"Walk in time," said Tobias. "Think of your map." He could see it in his head, Silver's Hallow Wood, the primaeval forest spilling off the edges of the paper. There was a time three thousand years gone you could have walked from one end of the country to the other never leaving the shadow of the trees. "The Green Man walks the wood," he tried explaining. "But the wood remembers."

Silver paused with an arrested expression. For a moment he stared pale-eyed into dawn-dim air, seeing something Tobias never would—maybe never had. Then he smiled faintly and nodded, just once.

But his expression as he glanced up to the Hall was still pained. "Mr Finch," he said.

"I thought it was *Tobias* now?"

"Mr Finch, I—"

"I know you picked a fight. But she's no ogress," said Tobias. "She had me cut down the old oak for you, and I'd never have had the strength to do it else. If not for her, Fabian would have swallowed you whole long since."

Silver opened his mouth to say something, but then he stopped, frowning, and came closer to Tobias instead. He put his hand on Tobias's arm, and then his other hand on Tobias's shoulder, and then he went up on his toes and kissed Tobias's lips.

He had a sweet, soft mouth. Nothing Tobias was used to. Fabian had been very different.

Ah, but Fabian had been very long ago.

He pushed Silver gently back after a moment. "What?" Silver said.

Tobias tilted his head towards the long green expanse of the lawn, and the small stiff figure waiting on the steps of the Hall. Silver turned and looked. He tried to hold on to Tobias's hand.

"No," said Tobias. "I'll come after."

"What *is* the point of all this if I can't at least hide behind you?" said Silver.

"Go," said Tobias.

Silver didn't try to wheedle, though he plainly wanted to. His fingers untangled from Tobias's reluctantly. Tobias watched him set off across the grass towards his waiting mother. He stayed where he was, leaning against the young tree that was the old walking stick. It was strong enough to take his full weight now. Not bad for a couple of seasons' growth.

He wasn't surprised when Bramble stepped out of nowhere and walked towards him. Small white flowers sprung up in her wake. She looked newly strange to Tobias's eyes, which had grown used to a year of ordinary people in their ordinary houses. Her eyes were a clear shining gold.

"He is not like the other one," she said.

"No," said Tobias. "Suppose not."

He only half meant it. Silver *was* like Fabian, a little; beautiful and clever, just as Fabian had been. Those things didn't mean much to Bramble, of course. She looked at the world with different eyes.

"He will be a good thing, here," she said. "He has planted himself."

"Like I did?" said Tobias.

"You were never planted here," said Bramble. "You were only stuck, like a rabbit in a—" She stopped. After a moment she made a face.

"A snare," Tobias supplied. "People thing, my dear."

"You loved us and we loved you," Bramble said. "But you never chose the wood. He did."

"Now then," said Tobias, who didn't remember it that way.

"He did," she insisted, and it seemed to make sense to her. Tobias looked away.

"You were a good thing also," said Bramble. "Go now and do people things. Then come back and do people things. Build and hunt. Set snares, cut paths. Plant more trees."

"And you, my dear?" Tobias said after a moment. "You should choose yourself a tree, you know. Plant yourself. Else you'll get peculiar."

"I *am* peculiar," said Bramble. "I chose already."

"Tell me where to visit you, then," said Tobias.

"Everywhere," she said simply. "Every tree. They're all mine." She held out her hand to Tobias and he saw it contained a sprig of mistletoe. "For hunting wickedness," Bramble said. "*Wickedness* is a people thing, but your friend told me a story and made me understand. There was wickedness in the wood before, but now it is gone, and I am glad. You were unhappy, but now you will not be, and I am glad." That was a lot of words at once for a dryad and Bramble looked rather shocked at herself. "Go," she managed. "Grow."

"I'll come back," Tobias said after a moment, "and do people things." He took the mistletoe and tucked it through his belt.

"Good," said Bramble. "He'll need you."

"You won't, though."

"No," she said patiently, "because I'm not a *people*. But I will still love you."

"You as well, my dear," Tobias said, after a moment when his throat felt too thick to speak. "You as well."

He knew the dryad was watching him go as he walked back to the Hall and the white room there. He felt the

wood behind him, four hundred years of the wood behind him. And as Silver waved him over and Mrs Silver
bestowed a thin smile on him he felt himself for a moment as the stump of a rotten old tree, putting up thin
green shoots at strange new angles.

Acknowledgments

With enormous thanks to:

My agent, Kurestin Armada, who encouraged me at every turn.

My editor, Ruoxi Chen, who understands tree jail.

The Tor.com Publishing team: production editor Lauren Hougen, copy editor Richard Shealy, proofreader Shveta Thakrar; David Curtis, who did the fantastic cover art, and Christine Foltzer, the art director; Irene Gallo, publisher and creative director; and Mordicai Knode, Caroline Perny, and Amanda Melfi, for their hard work on marketing, publicity, and social media.

Everina Maxwell, for years of writing chat.

Jennifer Mace, a staunch arboreal ally.

The Armada slack, a bastion of kindness and good sense.

The readers of the AO3 who read, kudosed, and commented on an earlier version of this story; it wouldn't exist without you!

The writers of the S2B2 archive, who have given me many good things to read over the years.

Mum, Dad, Paddy, and Oli, for everything.

Luke, for your love.

About the Author

EMILY TESH grew up in London and studied classics at Trinity College, Cambridge, followed by a master's degree in humanities at the University of Chicago. She now lives in Hertfordshire, where she passes her time teaching Latin and Ancient Greek to schoolchildren who have done nothing to deserve it. She has a husband and a cat. Neither of them knows any Latin yet, but it is not for lack of trying. *Silver in the Wood* is her first book.

TOR·COM

Science fiction. Fantasy. The universe. And related subjects.

*

More than just a publisher's website, *Tor.com* is a venue for **original fiction, comics,** and **discussion** of the entire field of SF and fantasy, in all media and from all sources. Visit our site today—and join the conversation yourself.